Dear Parent:
Your child's love of reading starts here!

Every child learns to read in a different way and at his or her own speed. Some go back and forth between reading levels and read favorite books again and again. Others read through each level in order. You can help your young reader improve and become more confident by encouraging his or her own interests and abilities. From books your child reads with you to the first books he or she reads alone, there are I Can Read Books for every stage of reading:

SHARED READING
Basic language, word repetition, and whimsical illustrations, ideal for sharing with your emergent reader

BEGINNING READING
Short sentences, familiar words, and simple concepts for children eager to read on their own

READING WITH HELP
Engaging stories, longer sentences, and language play for developing readers

READING ALONE
Complex plots, challenging vocabulary, and high-interest topics for the independent reader

ADVANCED READING
Short paragraphs, chapters, and exciting themes for the perfect bridge to chapter books

I Can Read Books have introduced children to the joy of reading since 1957. Featuring award-winning authors and illustrators and a fabulous cast of beloved characters, I Can Read Books set the standard for beginning readers.

A lifetime of discovery begins with the magical words **"I Can Read!"**

Visit www.icanread.com for information
on enriching your child's reading experience.

I Can Read Book® is a trademark of HarperCollins Publishers.

Library of Congress Control Number: 2016949892
ISBN 978-0-06-243080-9 (trade bdg.) — ISBN 978-0-06-243079-3 (pbk.)

Typography by Brenda E. Angelilli

17 18 19 20 21   SCP   10 9 8 7 6 5 4 3 2 1   ❖   First Edition

I Can Read!

BEGINNING 1 READING

PADDINGTON
at the Barber Shop

Michael Bond
illustrated by R. W. Alley

HARPER

An Imprint of HarperCollinsPublishers

Every morning Paddington
went to visit his good friend
Mr. Gruber at his shop.
They shared cocoa and buns
and caught up on the day's news.

One day Mr. Gruber

showed Paddington a vase.

A piece had broken off.

Paddington offered to fix the vase.

He put it in his basket on wheels

and went to buy some glue.

Along the way,
Paddington passed a shop
with a sign that read "Help Wanted."
He went inside.

It was a barber shop.

Mr. Sloop, the barber,

offered Paddington a job sweeping

and looking after the customers.

"Bears are good
at sweeping," Paddington said.
"If you do well, you can try
the clippers," Mr. Sloop replied.

Mr. Sloop showed Paddington
where to find the broom.
Then he went out for a coffee.
"I won't be long," he said.

Paddington looked around.

The shop was full

of interesting things.

He saw benches and newspapers.

He saw mirrors and chairs.

He looked at pictures

of different hairstyles.

He smelled shampoos and lotions.

Paddington picked up the scissors.

Snip, snip!

He almost cut his fur!

He put the scissors down again.

Paddington went back
to the closet.

Brooms, brushes, towels,
and a white coat fell out!

As Paddington untangled the items,
a bell rang.

A customer came into the shop.

He asked for a trim.

Paddington asked the customer

to wait for the barber.

But the man was tired

and in a hurry.

The man sat in the barber's chair.

Before Paddington could speak,

he had fallen asleep.

Paddington didn't know what to do.

But he knew he had

to keep the customers happy.

Paddington draped a cloth

around the man's shoulders.

Then he picked up

the clippers.

He waved the clippers a few times
in the air for practice.
Then he moved them
through the man's hair.

The first cut took all

of the man's hair off his head

in one swoop.

The man was almost bald.

Paddington sat down
on his suitcase to think.
Then he spotted a bottle
high up on the shelf.

It was hair-growing tonic.

Paddington poured it

on the man's head.

Paddington waited and waited
for the man's hair to grow.
He looked through his binoculars,
but there was still no hair.

At a loss, Paddington spotted

his shopping basket on wheels.

He put the vase on the counter

and took out a jar of marmalade.

He spread the marmalade
all over the man's head.
He took some hair from the floor
and put it on top.

Now the man's hair
was black and brown
and blond and red.
Paddington sighed in relief.

When the man woke up,
he was not happy.

Then he spotted Mr. Gruber's vase
and picked it up.

"That's Mr. Gruber's!"
Paddington cried.

The man was eager to see
more pieces just like the vase.

Paddington led the man

to Mr. Gruber's shop.

He bought many things there.

Mr. Gruber and Paddington shared

a late-day cocoa to celebrate.

"A very good day's work,"

Mr. Gruber said.

And Paddington had to agree.